The MIDNIGHT FEAST

Written by Lindsay Camp

Illustrated by Tony Ross

Ⓐ

Andersen Press • London

Text copyright © 1996 by Lindsay Camp. Illustrations copyright © 1996 by Tony Ross.
The rights of Lindsay Camp and Tony Ross to be identified as the author and illustrator of this work have been asserted by
them in accordance with the Copyright, Designs and Patents Act, 1988.
First published in Great Britain in 1996 by Andersen Press Ltd., 20 Vauxhall Bridge Road, London SW1V 2SA.
Published in Australia by Random House Australia Pty., 20 Alfred Street, Milsons Point, Sydney, NSW 2061. All rights
reserved. Colour separated in Switzerland by Photolitho AG, Offsetreproduktionen, Gossau, Zürich. Printed and bound
in Italy by Grafiche AZ, Verona.

10   9   8   7   6   5   4   3   2   1

British Library Cataloguing in Publication Data available.
ISBN 0 86264 684 7

This book has been printed on acid-free paper

At bathtime, Alice whispered something to Freddie.

What was that?

Nothing.

What is a midnight feast?

Shhhh!

"Night night, love," said Mum, stretching to kiss Alice in the top bunk.

"Night night, poppet," she said, bending to kiss Freddie in the bottom bunk.

As soon as Mum was gone,

Alice climbed out of bed.

Come on, we've got to get ready.

She pulled the quilt off Freddie's bed and spread it on the floor.

Alice took a plastic bag from under the bunks and looked inside.

We need some more food. I don't think beautiful princesses like salt and vinegar crisps.

What *do* they like?

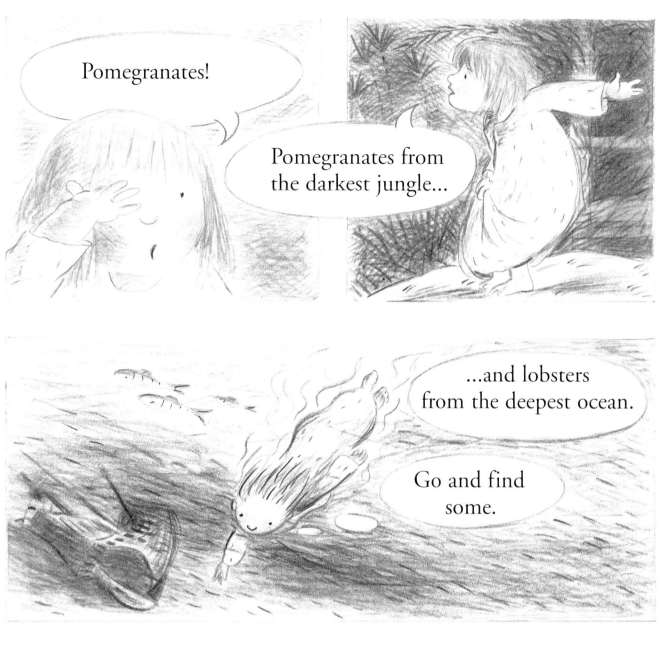

Freddie crept downstairs...

...and went to look for pomegranates and lobsters.

Mum was tidying the playroom...

...and he didn't think she heard him.

When Freddie got back, Alice was sitting on his quilt.

She took the lobsters and pomegranates from him.

Alice wriggled a bit on Freddie's quilt.

Freddie crept downstairs...

...and went to hunt for a soft golden cushion.

A floorboard creaked, but Mum was in the kitchen now...

...and she was humming to herself quite loudly.

When he got back, Alice was just making sure that one of the pomegranates was sweet enough.

Alice licked juice off her chin, and Freddie gave her the soft golden cushion.

I think beautiful princesses like music.

We need an enchanted musical box.

Go and find one.

Where?

Quickly, there isn't much time.

Freddie hurried downstairs, and nearly tripped over Beelzebub.

But Mum had turned on the TV...   ...so she didn't hear.

When Freddie got back, Alice was sitting on the soft golden cushion, licking one of the lobsters.

The last one.

Alice took the enchanted musical box from him.

Freddie sat down next to Alice...   ...and waited.

A few minutes passed.

Shall I go and look for some more pomegranates and lobsters before the beautiful princess comes?

It's all right. I don't think
she'll be very hungry.
And if she is, I suppose
she could eat the salt
and vinegar crisps.

Freddie waited some more.
"When will she come?" he yawned. "It must be midnight now."

But Alice didn't answer.

A little later, the door opened, and someone came in. She covered
Alice with a quilt, and kissed her. She lifted Freddie gently into bed
and covered him too. Then she kissed him. Freddie opened his
eyes for a moment.
"I knew you'd come," he whispered, "my sister said so."

And then Freddie closed his eyes and went back to sleep.

And dreamed all night of a beautiful princess
holding him in her arms.